I Love You AMERICANLY

By Lynn Parrish Sutton

Illustrated by
Melanie Hope Greenberg

Kane Miller
A DIVISION OF EDC PUBLISHING

I love you capitally like Washington, DC.

I love you tremendously like a
redwood tree.

I love you continuously like Seattle's rain.

I love you abundantly like the fruited plain.

I love you duckily like the Public Garden's flowers.

I love you impressively like Chicago's gleaming towers.

I love you colossally like the High Cascades.

I love you bountifully like the Everglades.

I love you majestically like the Sierra's rise.
I love you beautifully like the spacious skies.

I love you connectedly
like Chesapeake Bay.

I love you creatively
like snazzy LA.

I love you wondrously like the Blue Ridge Mountains.

I love you spectacularly like the Bellagio fountains.

I love you diversely like
the Texas Big Bend.

I love you strongly like
Tornado Alley's wind.

I love you endlessly like the Cape Cod sands.

I love you dramatically like the bare Badlands.

I love you intensely like Niagara Falls.

I love you immensely like the Grand Canyon's walls.

I love you magically like Monument Valley.

I love you musically like a Nashville alley.

I love you largely like the five Great Lakes.

I love you steadily like Denali's flakes.

I love you strikingly like the Golden Gate Bridge.

I love you astonishingly like a Rocky Mountain ridge.

I love you faithfully like Yellowstone's spout.

I love you curiously like Will Roger's Route.

I love you energetically like NYC.

I love you simply like the stark Mohave.

I love you anciently like the Southwestern ruins.

I love you greatly like the Colorado dunes.

I love you extensively like the Continental Divide.

I love you predictably like the North Atlantic tide.

I love you stunningly like the Pacific Coast Highway.

I love you protectively like the Outer Bank's flyway.

I love you welcomingly like the St. Louis Arch.

I love you permanently like Mt. Rushmore's granite art.

I love you historically like a Gettysburg mortar.

I love you jazzily like the French Quarter.

I love you declaratively like Independence Hall.

I love you joyously like the Derby's first call.

I love you lushly like a Hawaiian island
I love you inclusively like *your land* and *my land*.

I love you wholesomely like a warm apple pie.
I love you soaringly like a ninth inning fly.

I love you grandly like the wave of Old Glory.
I love you complexly like our national story.

I love you necessarily like sweet liberty.
I love you vastly like our growing country.